Inspiring WORDS

30 VERSES FROM THE BIBLE YOU CAN COLOR

ZONDERVAN

ZONDERVAN

Inspiring Words

Copyright © 2015 by Zondervan

This book is also available as a Zondervan ebook.
Visit www.zondervan/ebooks.

Requests for information should be addressed to:

Zonderkidz, 3900 *Sparks Dr. SE, Grand Rapids, Michigan* 49546

ISBN 978-0-310-75728-3

Type design: Micah Kandros
Editor: Jacque Alberta
Design: Cindy Davis

Printed in the United States

15 16 17 18 /PHP/ 23 22 21 20 19 18 17 16 15 14 13 12 11 10 9 8 7 6 5 4

THIS BOOK
BELONGS TO
HEATHER

Take Delight in the Lord, & He Will Give You the Desires of Your Heart.

Psalm 37:4

THE LORD'S WORD IS FLAWLESS; HE SHIELDS ALL WHO TAKE REFUGE IN HIM.

2 SAMUEL 22:31

One
WHO HAS
UNRELIABLE
FRIENDS
SOON COMES TO
RUIN,
but there is a
FRIEND
WHO STICKS
CLOSER THAN A
BROTHER.
Proverbs 18:24

So the Last will be first, & the first will be last.
Matthew 20:16

AND THE *Lord* HAS DECLARED THIS *Day* THAT *You* ARE HIS *People*, *His* TREASURED POSSESSION *as He* PROMISED, AND THAT *You are* TO KEEP ALL HIS COMMANDS.

Deuteronomy 26:18

BECAUSE YOUR HEART WAS ← RESPONSIVE & YOU HUMBLED YOURSELF BEFORE THE Lord... I ALSO HAVE HEARD YOU, DECLARES THE Lord.

2 KINGS 22:19

The LORD is my strength and my defense; he has become my salvation. He is my GOD, and I will praise him, my father's GOD, and I will exalt him.

Exodus 15:2

DECLARE
THE PRAISES
OF HIM
WHO CALLED
YOU OUT
OF DARKNESS
INTO HIS
WONDERFUL
LIGHT.
1 PETER 2:9

BUT GOD SENT ME AHEAD OF YOU TO PRESERVE FOR YOU A REMNANT ON EARTH & TO SAVE YOUR LIVES BY A GREAT DELIVERANCE.

GENESIS 45:7

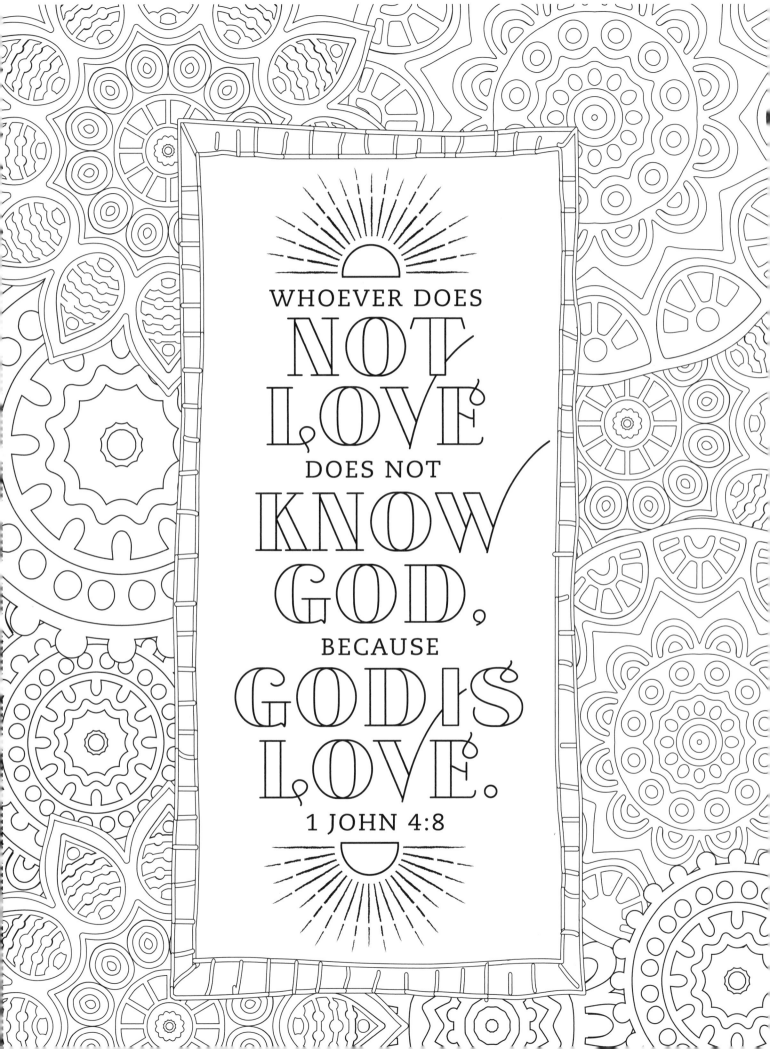

WHOEVER DOES
NOT
LOVE
DOES NOT
KNOW
GOD,
BECAUSE
GOD IS
LOVE.
1 JOHN 4:8

Therefore, IF ANYONE IS IN *Christ,* THE NEW *creation* HAS COME: THE OLD *has gone,* THE *New* IS HERE!

2 Corinthians 5:17

Love
L the
Lord
your
God
with all
your
Heart
& with
all
your
Soul
& with
all
your
Mind.
Matthew 22:37

THE PRAYER OF A RIGHTEOUS PERSON IS POWER-FUL & effective.
JaMes 5:16

FOR
IN
HIM
*all
THINGS
were
CREATED.
Colossians 1:16

I have come that they may have Life, & have it to the Full.

John 10:10

THERE IS
NO ONE
ON EARTH LIKE
HIM; HE
IS BLAMELESS &
UPRIGHT,
A MAN WHO
FEARS
GOD &
SHUNS
EVIL.
JOB 2:3